BOISTEROUS BILLY
by TONY GARTH

When Billy got excited, he became very boisterous indeed.

He just couldn't help himself. He liked being noisy and he liked running fast. He liked it a lot. What Billy didn't realise was that other people didn't always share his high spirits.

Billy was always the loudest boy in the class. His voice boomed out above all the rest. It made his teacher very cross.

Once he was boisterous at a wedding and upset the bride.

He was noisy in the cinema and disturbed the other people in the audience. Eventually, he was asked to leave.

He was boisterous at his Aunty's house. He knocked over the coffee table and spilt all the biscuits.

Billy's Mum was very angry with him.

"There's a time and a place for being noisy and running fast," she told him. "But it's not in the classroom, and it's not at a wedding, and it's not at the cinema and it's certainly not at your Aunty's."

Next day, Billy went shopping with his Mum. First stop was the supermarket. Billy loved to whizz up and down the aisles with the shopping trolley.

As Billy charged up to the trolley park, his Mum shouted after him.

"Remember what I said, Billy," she warned. "There's a time and a place for everything."

Billy grabbed a trolley. He was about to set off at top speed.

"Is it now?" he shouted to his Mum.

Billy's Mum shook her head.

So, Billy calmly pushed the trolley up and down each aisle, waiting quietly for his Mum to fill it.

But it wasn't nearly as much fun as tearing about and Billy could feel the excitement starting to bubble up inside him. He couldn't wait to find the time and the place. He hoped it would be soon.

Next, Billy and his Mum went to pick up some dry-cleaning.

"Is it now?" he yelled, jumping up and down.

"Shhh!" said his Mum. "No, it isn't."

Billy waited patiently for his Mum to pay, but the bubble of excitement inside him was growing all the time. He began to feel quite dizzy.

By the time they got home, Billy was almost bursting with excitement.

"Dad's home!" he shrieked. "Look, Dad's home. Is it now? Is it now?"

His Mum laughed.

"Nearly," she said.

Remembering what his Mum had told him, Billy tried not to run down the garden path. He managed a fast walk instead. But he couldn't contain his excitement much longer...

He barged through the front door.

"Dad! Dad! We're home," he yelled.

"Is it now?" he asked, more quietly.

"Yes, Billy," his Dad said. "It's now. Now is the time and the place to be boisterous. But it must be in the back garden."

Billy was a bit disappointed. He could be boisterous anytime he liked in the back garden, But it wasn't much fun on his own.

Billy went into the garden. But things just weren't the same somehow. He didn't have the energy to run anywhere. He couldn't even be bothered to shout.

Then, suddenly, a huge, furry ball came lolloping down the garden path.

"Woof!" it said, as it knocked Billy flying.

"Woof! Woof!" it continued, as it licked his face.

Billy was very surprised.

"My very own boisterous dog," he said, laughing and patting the furry ball's head.

"Come on, boy," he shouted, at the top of his voice.

The dog barked and barked and Billy whooped and yelled as they played together noisily, ran very fast and were extremely boisterous. It was difficult to tell which one was worse!

Look out for the next six Little Monsters!

HELPFUL
HENRY

SHY
SOPHIE

BOSSY
BETHANY

REVOLTING
RONNIE

WORRIED
WINNIE

TV TREVOR